1.25p

KIDNAPPING
at
BELVOIR CASTLE

by Molly Burkett

Illustrations by Vivienne Kenney
for William, Oliver & Christine.

Chapter One

The five boys made a dash for the coach when it arrived outside the school gates. They wanted to sit on the back seat. Mrs Dixon was there first however and she made them stand back while the girls got on first.

"Silly old fool," Billy muttered.

"What was that you said, Billy Bennet?" Mrs Dixon asked.

"Nothing, miss," he said nudging his friend.

Two girls were sitting on the back seat when the boys did get on but they soon pushed them off. Mrs Dixon didn't notice. She was busy checking the names off her list.

"Elizabeth Marks."

"Yes miss."

"Jenny Nolan."

"Yes miss."

"Carol Pearce."

"Here Mrs Dixon."

"Samantha Simpson...... Samantha Simpson... has anyone seen Samantha, oh, there you are. Do try and use your ears, dear, instead of your mouth. Emma Smith, do wake up Emma. No dear, don't start your sandwiches now. Keep

1

them for lunchtime. You've only just had your breakfast."

"I don't know why she keeps telling us to be quiet when she never stops talking herself," Billy grumbled.

When Mrs Dixon was satisfied that they were all sitting properly, she took her seat next to Mr Clark, telling the driver that he could start. The children started waving to the parents who had come to see them off. The coach hadn't gone more than a few yards when Mrs Dixon ordered it to stop. Her voice was so commanding that the driver put his foot on the brake immediately. The coach stopped so suddenly that some of the children fell off their seats.

"Who's left their jacket on the school gate?" she called out.

"You again Billy Bennet. I don't know why I trouble to ask. Go and get it. I suppose those are your sandwiches too. You'd forget your head if it was loose. What's that you've got in your hand. I'll take care of that. We won't be needing any guns at Belvoir Castle."

Mrs Dixon reached out and took the gun from Billy's hand. She must have pressed the trigger at the same time because a jet of water squirted out of it and it hit her full in the face. Water ran down her face and down the front of her clothes. She dropped the gun and vigorously tried to brush the water away.

"You stupid boy," she exclaimed. "Why didn't you tell me it was a water pistol. Now look at my clothes. I'm soaked through."

Billy hurried to the back of the coach, his friends were giggling at the sight of Mrs Dixon mopping up the water.

"Silly old fool," Billy muttered.

"What was that you said, Billy Bennet?" Mrs Dixon called out.

"Nothing miss," Billy said.

The five boys knelt on the back seat, looking out of the rear window, seeing who could make the ugliest face at the drivers of the cars coming up behind them. Most of the drivers ignored them, but some made faces back at them. Then

2

Shaun thought of some signs they could make. That was when the coach stopped suddenly again. There was a police car in front of them and Mrs Dixon went to the coach door to talk to one of the policemen. Then she turned and looked at the children. Her eyes rested on the five boys sitting on the back seat. The boys were facing her, looking as innocent as babies.

"Billy Bennet," she said, "are you making signs at the drivers behind the coach? I would have thought even you would have had enough sense not to do that to a police car. You'd better come and sit down here, near me, where I can keep an eye on you. Come along."

"You didn't tell me they were rude signs," Billy said to Shaun.

The coach had only just started up again when one of the girls called out, "There's the castle."

And there it was. Belvoir Castle stood out, proud and clear, dominating the wooded slopes beneath it. As the coach drew nearer, clouds gathered behind the turrets and the castle walls grew dark and forbidding. The feeling transferred itself to the children and they became silent as they approached the castle, almost hypnotised by the fantastic building. There was something magnificent and awe inspiring about that castle, but there was something frightening about it too.

Chapter Two

The children were quiet as they walked up to the castle, silenced by those dark, awe inspiring walls. Mrs Dixon wasn't. She never stopped talking and because the five boys were the last off the coach, she walked up behind them.

"Look at your shoe-laces David Wright. You'll be falling flat on your face if you don't watch out. Emma dear, don't eat your sandwiches now. They're for your lunch. Just look where you're going Samantha, you nearly knocked that gentleman right off the path......"

"What's that wriggling in your pocket, Billy Bennet?" Joanne asked.

"Oh, that's Henry."

"What've you brought him for?" Shaun said.

"Henry wants a trip out now and again, same as we do. Besides, it's not a him, it's a her. She had five babies."

"You haven't brought those too, have you?" asked Joanne

"No, of course I haven't. I sold those to the pet shop down Silver Street."

"Well you'd better not let old Mother Dixon see it. She'd have a fit if she thought there were thirty six children and a hamster in the group."

A guide met them at the entrance to the castle. Mrs Dixon fussed around getting them into order. Mr Clark took his pipe from his mouth, said "Quiet" and put it back in his mouth again. He only ever said one word to Mrs Dixon's thousand but the children did what he told them straight away.

The guide lead them through into the Guard room.

"Cor," said Billy. He and his friends stared round them in wonder. It was a magnificent high ceilinged room, but it wasn't the architecture that impressed the boys. It was the weapons that lined the walls that held their attention. Rows of guns lead into the room while swords and flags and suits of armour surrounded them. The guide was telling them all about the history of the castle but the boys hardly listened to her, they were so fascinated by all the weapons.

"Don't you touch a thing," Mrs Dixon's voice rang out, as Billy's finger stretched out towards one of the guns.

The guide was talking about the weapons now and Billy was imagining the battles in which they could have been used, seeing the knights in their armour and the soldiers wielding their swords.

"There's a mouse," Mrs Dixon screamed hysterically, looking back towards the row of guns. "It's a mouse, I tell you it's a mouse. It ran under that seat there. I tell you, I saw it."

Even the guide was silenced by her outburst.

"I've never seen a mouse in the castle..." the guide started.

"It was a mouse," Mrs Dixon said firmly, recovering her composure." I saw it quite clearly."

"I'll report it to the manager," the guide said and started to herd the party upstairs.

"Lord," said Billy, feeling in his pockets, "it's Henrietta. She's eaten right through my pocket. I better go and find her." He ran back to where Mrs Dixon said she had seen the mouse. He got on his hands and knees and crawled along the floor, calling Henrietta's name as loud as he dared. He was the only person in this great hall and none would have heard him had

5

"There's a mouse" screamed Mrs Dixon.

6

he shouted but there was something about the place that made you want to keep your voice down. Billy spoke in little more than a whisper.

The children were in one of the bedrooms when Billy caught up with them.

"Have you got her?" Shaun asked.

Billy nodded and patted his pocket. "She bit my finger," he said indignantly.

Mrs Dixon had seen him come in and she sidled round the group until she had reached him.

"What are you up to now?" she said. "I think you'd better stay close to me while we're going round the castle. I'll keep my eye on you, my boy."

Mrs Dixon kept at the back of the group to make sure none of the children were left behind, so she and Billy trailed behind the others. As the guide told them more and more about the castle and its contents, Billy became more and more fascinated and he kept stopping to look at things. Mrs Dixon kept urging him to keep up.

He first noticed the man when they were going through the ballroom. Billy had stopped to look at the costumes in a glass case. The rest of the group had moved into the next room. Billy was looking carefully at the costumes when a figure in one of the cases seemed to move. Billy held his breath for a minute, wondering if he had seen a ghost, then the figure moved again and he realised it was someone on the other side of the glass cases. There was something about him that made Billy stay quite still. His face was slightly distorted by the thickness of glass through which the boy could see him, but it wasn't his appearance that made Billy wary, it was the way he moved. There was something sinister about the way he looked round the door, the way he walked cautiously into the room - looked up and saw Billy. For a few seconds the two of them stared at each other through the glass cases. Then he turned and shuffled hurriedly out of the room.

He seemed to be following them. Billy saw him look round the door when they were in the bedroom with the white

Something warned Billy to stay still.

and gold drapes hanging over the old fashioned bed. Billy caught another glimpse of him in one of the long gilt mirrors in the dining room. Billy swung round to look at the place where the man must be, but he had disappeared once again.

"Who's that old man in carpet slippers who's following us around?" he asked Mrs Dixon.

"Sh...," she replied, "I think it must be the duke."

"He doesn't look much like a duke to me," Billy said.

Billy didn't take much notice of the man again, not until they had made their way through the last of the beautifully furnished rooms, the Regent's Gallery, and he wouldn't have seen him then if Henrietta hadn't started to play up. The hamster would not settle down in Billy's pocket. Billy took her out, held her on the palm of his hand and gave her a serious talk, but she still wriggled and squirmed when Billy put her back in his pocket. He was following the rest of the group through the door, out of the gallery when he heard a small thump. He knew what it was straight away. He didn't need to put his hand in his pocket to discover that Henrietta was no longer there. She had eaten her way through that one too. He lunged forwards to catch hold of the small animal but the hamster was too quick for him. She ran back the way they had just come. Billy threw himself full length on the ground after her and just managed to catch hold of one of her back legs. Carefully he pulled her towards him. He was just beginning to get up when his attention was caught by a movement reflected in the mirror above him. The man was there again but it took Billy a second or two to realise exactly where he was because the whole of the end wall was a mirror and the smaller mirror above his head caught his reflection and returned it to the mirrored wall, so Billy could not only see one man, he saw images of four or five. As the man moved, it seemed to Billy that several identical men were moving and then all the shapes moved into one and there was just the one man there, the man that had been following the school group round the castle, the man that Mrs. Dixon thought was the duke.

The man was looking round and there was a furtive look on his face. Something warned Billy to stay still and he lay full length on the floor holding firmly on to the hamster's back leg, hardly daring to breathe.

"If I can see him in the mirror, he'll be able to see me," Billy thought, but if the man could see him, he didn't take any notice of the boy. Then Billy realized that, because he was on the floor, it was unlikely that the mirror would show up his reflection. Billy forgot all about that as he watched the man. He looked round the gallery and stood there as if he was listening for something. The only thing that could be heard were the voices of the children growing steadily dimmer as they went further away from the gallery, then they could be heard no longer and the room was silent, completely silent.

The hamster chose that moment to try and escape. Billy held on to her hind leg even more firmly, frightened that the scratching sounds she was making on the floor would alert the duke, but he didn't seem to hear. He grunted with satisfaction and went back, out of the gallery, only to return a few seconds later with a sack over his shoulder. Billy could see by the way he was carrying it, that it must be heavy. He put the sack down and reached up to one of the candle sticks and started to remove it.

"He's stealing it," Billy thought. "Why would a duke want to steal his own candle sticks?"

The duke held the candlestick in front of his face and the light reflected against the silver and made patterns on his skin. He laughed out loud and dropped it into his sack. Billy heard the clink as it dropped against other articles. Then the duke bent down and started pushing and pulling at something on the ground. Billy couldn't see the man himself but he could see his reflection in the mirror and it looked as though he was doing physical jerks, bending down and touching his toes one, two, three, four, five times as he was reflected from the glass wall and back to the mirror many times over. Billy was puzzled. Whatever was the man doing? Then he saw that the duke was lifting the carpet, folding the corner right back.

He put his bag on the ground and started to finger the candle stick.

11

Surely he wasn't trying to steal his own carpet too.

Then Billy saw that something was happening to the wall, the end wall that was one huge mirror. A crack was appearing across it, starting at the floor and working its way upwards. Then the most peculiar thing happened that Billy had ever seen in his life. The man dropped the carpet back in place, walked through the mirror and disappeared. The crack across the glass went too and once again the end wall looked like one huge mirror. Billy was so astonished by what he had seen that he let go of the hamster and sat up, rubbing his eyes to make sure that he really was seeing right.

It must have taken Billy five minutes to catch the hamster again. He emptied out his sandwich box, put the hamster in that and gave her half a cheese sandwich for company. Then he turned his attention to the corner of the room where he had seen the man disappear. He put his bag on the ground and looked at the glass wall. How could the duke have walked through that? He folded back the carpet and looked at the floor boards. There was nothing unusual there except that a knot of wood seemed to stick out. He bent down and touched it. It wobbled. It was loose. As Billy handled it, it began to turn, to unscrew. Immediately the crack in the mirror began to appear again, only now Billy could see that it wasn't a crack at all. It was a door sliding slowly and silently open. revealing another mirror behind it, so that from a distance, it would have been difficult to see that there was an opening there at all.

"That's how he disappeared," Billy thought, taking a step inside the door to see where the man had gone. As he stepped through the mirror, the door slid silently shut behind him, cutting him off from the light, imprisoning him in the small, dark cupboard. He had thrown himself at the door before it finally shut, trying to catch hold of the door edge, trying to pull it back, but he was not strong enough to hold it, the door slid firmly shut. Frantically Billy tried to slide the door open again, to push it back, but he made no impression on it at all. If twisting a knot in the floor board had opened it from the outside, perhaps there was another trick that would open it from the inside. He felt his way round the cupboard, pushing every uneven stone, trying to turn anything that protruded from the wall, but it was no use. The door remained firmly closed. He was shut in a big box and no-one would know where he was. He felt the panic rising in him. Then he remembered the man. He had come through this way and he was no longer there. There must be another way out. Once again he started to feel round the walls of the cupboard, moving systematically now. It was when he felt round on the floor that he felt the step and the hole above it, a hole that would only have allowed one man through at a time and he would have to bend very low to get through.

As soon as Billy was through the hole, the steps widened and he could stand upright. Carefully he leaned against the wall, feeling his way downwards. He knew that he was moving in a spiral, going round and round and down and down. He went slowly because the steps were uneven. Then there was a handrail and Billy held on to it thankfully. At the same time, he realised the dark was not as intense as it had been when he came through the sliding door. He wondered if his eyes were adapting to the darkness, but no, there was definitely light reaching the spiraling staircase from below. Billy went even more slowly now. The steps were leading somewhere but where. What would he find at the end of the staircase?

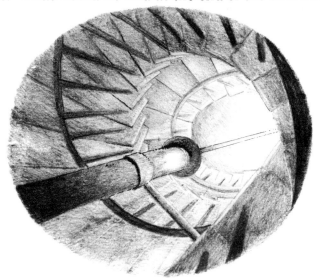

Chapter Three

The rest of the group had seen round the old kitchens and the beer cellars and were settling down to eat their lunch in one of the rooms beneath the castle. Mrs Dixon was busy sorting out the worksheets for the children and gave them to Joanne to hand round.

"There's one left," Joanne said handing it back to her.

"There can't be, they're exactly right. I counted them out myself," Mrs Dixon told her firmly. "There's the exact number of papers there."

"Perhaps there aren't the exact number of children," Mr Clark said.

That was when Mrs Dixon started counting through the list of children. She sent someone out to see if there was anyone in the toilets. Then she started going through the names. She didn't have to go very far.

"It's Billy Bennet that's missing," she stated. "I might have known it would be him. I don't know, why can't he be like all the other children. Has anyone seen Billy Bennet?" she called out.

Mr Clark took the unlit pipe from his mouth.

"Go and get him, Shaun," he said. Shaun left his

sandwiches and went to look for his friend.

It wasn't until they were packing up and getting ready to leave the room that Mrs Dixon commented that the two boys still weren't back. Mr. Clark looked cross. "I'll go and fetch them myself," he said, "they needn't think they're going to start playing these sort of tricks."

He was back in about twenty minutes to see if the boys had returned.

"I've been right round the public part of the castle," he said, "where the children have been and there isn't a sign of them. They can't simply disappear. I'm going to have this place searched."

It was almost an hour before he returned. The children had begun to get noisy and impatient and cross with Billy for making them hang around like this. Mr Clark signalled for Mrs Dixon to go outside with him.

"They're not in the castle. The staff have been helping me search. We've even been in the duke's private rooms. I'll swear those boys aren't in the building but they can't simply disappear. I've a feeling there's something funny going on. For one thing we're the only people here. It seems they don't usually have people visiting on a Friday but they made a mistake when they took our booking and they didn't cancel it because they didn't want to disappoint the children. There's very few staff on duty either but the man who helped me look for the boys said he thought there were some things missing."

"Swords, I suppose, or guns," Mrs Dixon interrupted. "That would be Billy Bennet. I've one of his guns here, or I did have. Wherever have I put it," and she started sorting through her handbag.

"No, it's nothing like that. The weapons are all there but a picture's been taken from the wall and some silver has gone."

"Billy wouldn't have anything to do with that. The boy's honest, he just doesn't think."

"It's a maze of passages downstairs but the men went

right through them. I went down to the coach myself to see if they'd got lost and gone back there but the driver hadn't seen them and that's the only way out, so they must be on the premises somewhere. They must be hiding out in the grounds. We don't even know that the two boys are together."

"Shaun would have come back when you told him. I think we'd better phone the school to let them know."

"That's just it," Mr Clark said, "I've tried and there's no outside line working. They've got an internal line and that's alright but they can't contact anyone outside. And there's another thing I don't like. There's hardly anyone on the premises. Seems they've only got a skeleton staff on. There can't be more than four or five people on the place except for us."

"And the duke."

"Oh yes, and the duke, but they couldn't find him either. There's something mighty odd going on."

"There's somebody looking out of the window, up there, look. He's staring at us."

"All the time I was looking for the boys, I felt someone was looking at me. I don't like this at all."

"What should we do."

"We'll get the children outside for a start, get some games going. We better behave as normal as possible."

Meanwhile Shaun had gone back to the room where he had last seen Billy. He found his friend's bag in the corner of the room, but there was no sign of Billy. He looked in the bag and found the sandwich box with the hamster inside happily eating the cheese sandwich. "Well, Billy wouldn't dump his pet and go off and leave him," Shaun thought. "He can't be far away."

He looked round the adjoining rooms but they were all completely empty. There was no sign that Billy had gone through any of them. He called Billy's name and whistled in the way that he usually did when he wanted his friend's attention but there was no answer, just the echo of his own

16

"There's somebody looking out of the window, up there, look."

17

voice being caught up in the corners of those huge rooms and coming back to him from every direction. Shaun stood beside Billy's bag and wondered what to do. There was not a sound. It was completely silent. The place was so quiet, so still, that Shaun began to feel uneasy. He wished one of the others had come with him, it wouldn't have felt so bad then. The way the room was reflected six or seven times in the mirrored wall made him feel unsettled and when he moved, every movement was reflected six or seven times too and he seemed to be in the company of six or seven identical boys, but when he turned away from that glass wall, he saw that he was very much on his own. It was as he turned away from the mirror that he saw the carpet had been moved. There was a line of unpolished wood showing where the edge of the carpet had been. It looked out of place in the carefully arranged room. He knelt down and folded the carpet back. It felt stiff to the touch but it folded back easily. Shaun had half expected to find a trap door, or some loose floorboards or something to let him know where his friend was, but there was nothing, just parallel lines of worn floor boards, then he noticed some dusty lines as if fingers had been scratched across the wood and they led to a knot raised a little from the surface. Billy must have made those marks. Shaun twisted the knot as he put his hand down. He hadn't twisted it on purpose, it was just one of those things, but it had the most peculiar effect. There was a whirring noise, only a faint noise but it sounded very loud in the empty, silent room. At the same time, a crack appeared across the mirror. Shaun swung round at the sound behind him. He stared with amazement at the hole in the glass wall, slowly being revealed as the door slid back.

"A secret passage," he breathed.

He took a step forward to see where the hole led and as he went over the threshold, into the cupboard, the door slid silently shut behind him. As the cupboard darkened, Shaun swung round and tried to escape before the opening disappeared completely, but he was too late. The gap was too narrow. He couldn't squeeze through it and then he was caught, imprisoned in the small dark cupboard.

Shaun didn't panic. He was too shocked for that. He knew that Billy must have found the secret door. He knew Billy could not be far away. If there was one secret door into this place, there was very likely a second one leading out of it. Carefully, he felt round the walls in the same way that Billy had done. That was how he found the steps leading downwards. He started down them.

"This is great," he thought, "a real secret passage." He thought about shouting to let Billy know he was following him, then he decided he wouldn't. He would creep up behind his friend and give him the surprise of his life. It was a good job he did make that decision.

Two men were talking in the room on the other side of the door.

Billy had reached the bottom of the steps and paused there wondering which way to go. There was a dark tunnel like passage leading away on his left and there was a partially open door on his right. Two men were talking in the room on the other side of the door. Their conversation made Billy stop still and listen.

"So," a deep, foreign voice spat out the word, "you come at last. I wait here for one hour."

"I couldn't help it," another voice replied. "There's a party of school kids and they took their time going round the place. There wasn't supposed to be anyone here today but they made a mistake with the booking."

"Mistakes, mistakes," the foreign voice rose to almost a scream. "We want no mistakes."

"Well, I'm here now and I've got us some loot." And there was the sound of metal tipping on to the floor.

"You fool, you stupid fool," the foreign voice had risen to a high pitched scream. "We have not come here for loot. We have not come here to steal. If someone sees these things have gone, they will come searching for us and that will be the end of all our plans. You are being paid good. You have no need of this...this loot."

"Too good a chance to miss, mate. It was there for the taking so I took it. I'll get a few bob for this little lot. So I'll have something to fall back on, won't I, if something goes wrong with your little scheme."

"Nothing will go wrong, do you hear me, nothing. It is sorted out how do you say, to the last degree. If anything did go wrong, it would only be through doing something stupid, like taking something we don't need and drawing the attention to ourselves."

"I had a close shave up there, I can tell you. There was this woman with all those kids kept looking at me like. If she'd come any nearer, she'd have seen my make up. Then she'd have known I wasn't the real duke."

"I keep telling you there is no worry. You look so like the old man that no-one could tell you apart. Even his own wife wouldn't know the difference. That is why you have been selected for this job."

"How is the duke, by the way. He didn't give you any trouble did he?"

"He gave me very much trouble. When he realised he had been tricked to come down here, he shout and he fight but he is quiet now. We give him a little injection."

"He ain't hurt, is he? You promised me no-one would get hurt. I don't want anything to do with this if anyone's going to get hurt."

"He is not hurt," the foreign man said. "He sleeps. Go and look at the old chap if you don't believe me."

There was silence for a few seconds, then the bogus duke said, "He looks alright, but I don't want him hurt. And you needn't bother about people looking for those few things I've taken because there isn't anyone about to notice. The duke suddenly became generous,didn't he, gave them all the afternoon off being as we were so slack. They went off more quickly than they would have done if a bomb had been planted in the place. There's only our lot up there now and those school kids but they'll be packing up and going well before four o'clock."

The foreigner chuckled, a deep, evil sound that came from the base of his throat.

"That was good thinking. We have the place to ourselves. Nothing can get in our way now," and there was such a note of evil satisfaction in his voice that Billy felt a shiver of apprehension run down his spine.

"So that's what they're up to," he thought. "I knew that man wasn't a duke. He didn't look like a duke. I must get help. I must let people know they've kidnapped the real duke," and he started to back carefully, trying not to make a sound, hardly daring to breathe in case the two men in the room knew he was there.

The rough hand thrust in front of his mouth gave him such a shock that he didn't have the chance to cry out. At the same time he was seized by the arms and frog marched into the room where the two men were talking. He struggled to break away from the grasp but he didn't have a chance. He was held as tightly as a mouse in a trap. Kicking and struggling, he was forced through the door and dropped onto a rug in the middle of the room. He had not expected the man to release him like that and he fell headlong onto the floor, in front of the two men.

"Look what I've found, hiding behind the door and listening to every word you've been saying."

The two men who had been talking inside the room stared at him with surprise. Billy struggled to his feet and looked back at them.

"So," the foreign man said, "so, you find us and now, my young man, you tell us how you find us."

There was something about the man's voice that frightened Billy, but he was determined not to let these men see. He stood there staring at the man, not attempting to answer.

"That's the boy who kept looking at me, the one who was with that woman at the back of the school children, the one I told you about," the man who was acting the part of the duke interrupted.

The man who had questioned Billy stared steadily at the boy.

"Who are you boy?" he spat out and there was something about the way he said those words that compelled Billy to answer. He didn't attempt to lie to him.

"Billy Bennet," he said, "I'm with the children from Huntingtower Road School and they'll be looking for me if I'm late back, so you'd better show me the way out."

"He's right you know," the acting duke said. "They will be looking for him. We'd better let him go."

"No." There was no mistaking the venom on that one word. "No, the boy stays here. Already he knows too much but first there are some things we must know. How did you find us here boy, how?" and his face came close to Billy's as he asked the question.

Billy shut his mouth stubbornly.

22

"Come on, boy. I mean to know."

Still Billy did not answer. With one movement, the man caught hold of his arm, and, turning him round, twisted it up his back. Billy winced with pain.

"How?" the man demanded and when Billy still did not answer, he jerked the arm again until the boy cried out.

"How," he repeated.

"I followed him through the hole in the wall," he said, nodding to the man who had stolen the silver. "I saw him carrying that sack on his back and I thought he was stealing the duke's silver, so I followed him."

The man flung Billy away and turned his attention on the plump man that Billy had followed. His voice quivered with anger and there was such a look of fury on his face that the 'duke' backed away from him and cowered against the wall.

"It is your greed that will ruin our plans," the man screamed at him, his foreign accent becoming more and more marked. "If you had not the sack, the boy would not have followed. Now we have an old man and a young boy that must be dealt with."

"You mustn't hurt him," the man who was acting as the duke said. "I don't want him hurt. I don't want anyone hurt. That was part of the agreement. You promised..."

"You have no right for promise. You are being well paid. You have much money for your part."

"I don't want anyone hurt," the man muttered.

Billy had tried to work his way towards the door. The two men were so concerned with their argument that they seemed to have forgotten him, but he soon came to a halt, caught against the feet of the man who had found him.

"The boy's right though," this man said. "They will be looking for him."

The foreign man swung round to face the boy. "Does anyone know where you are?"

"I...I don't know," Billy stammered.

"Of course they don't. They would have come and

23

fetched him by now if they had." The 'duke' had recovered his composure. He was dragging along behind the rest of the children all the time. That woman kept coming back to fetch him and telling him to keep up with the others. I bet they haven't even noticed he's gone, not yet, but I'll go back up and have a look round to make sure. I'll go up anyway and make sure that door shut properly behind him," and he started for the door.

Shaun drew back against the wall in horror. He had heard everything that the men had said. He had seen Billy captured and dragged into the room. He had just started on the last bend of the stairs when he saw Billy. He was about to run down the last few steps and leap on his friend's back but something about Billy's concentration, the way he stood, made him hesitate. It was at that moment he had seen the figure creeping from the dark tunnel. He was advancing on Billy so silently, so stealthily, Shaun opened his mouth to shout a warning to his friend, better still, he'd throw the bag at the man and he started to ease it from his shoulder, but he didn't have time. The man who had been advancing on Billy, like a cat stalking a mouse, suddenly sprang. He had Billy in his grasp and, kicking the door open, he carried the struggling boy into the room. It had all happened so quickly that Shaun had not had the chance to move. He stood there transfixed.

Now this man was coming back up the stairs. He would find him too. Shaun pressed himself against the wall. Carefully he started to creep backwards, up the spiraling staircase. He must fetch help but there was no time. The men were coming out of the room. Shaun forgot all caution now. He was running, scrambling back up those stairs, using his hands as well as his feet, to help him go faster. Twice, he nearly slipped and fell. Once he stopped to regain his breath and he knew then that the man was not far behind him. He could hear his footsteps echoing up the stairs. Breathless and panting, Shaun reached the dark cupboard like room that was behind the mirrored wall and flung himself at the sliding door, trying to force his fingers into the crack, attempting to ease the doors apart but they would not move. Desperately he battled with the doors but they stayed firmly shut. There was nothing he could do. He was caught like a rat in a trap. He could hear the man's footsteps getting closer and closer, hear his breath wheezing as he came higher up the steep stairs. Shaun flung himself at the door in one last attempt to get free, but it was no good. He was imprisoned. He drew back into the corner of the cupboard and sat on the floor, listening to the man coming closer, and waited.

Shaun forgot all caution now. He was running, scrambling back up those stairs.

25

Chapter Four

Shaun never could understand how the fat man failed to see him. He heard the man getting nearer and nearer as he climbed the spiral staircase and he had struggled to try and force the door open without success. He thought there was no hope for him and had drawn back into the corner of that dark cupboard and waited, pulling his anorak hood over his face. There was just a chance, a remote chance, that his dark clothes would merge with the darkness of the small room, just a chance that he would not be seen. Then he saw the light flash round the walls and knew that the man was carrying a powerful torch. The hope that he would escape detection was very slim.

The man had come up the last few steps, puffing and panting, stopping to rest on every other step. Then he had reached the entrance to the room. He did not come right in, but flashed the single beamed torch round the walls. The light travelled right over Shaun but it didn't stop. The man swung it round the room again. He gave a satisfied grunt and started to descend the stairs.

Shaun was astounded. Then he was jubilant. He hadn't seen him. The man hadn't seen him. Then his jubilation gave way to common sense. Even if the man had not seen him, the respite was only temporary. He had to get hep for Billy before he himself was found. He had to get that door open. He had to escape from that prison. Systematically he started working his way round the room, pressing, pulling, twisting anything that protruded from the wall. After a while he began to feel dizzy. It was difficult moving round in such complete darkness. He could feel the thread wide crack where the door had shut and tried to force it open but it was no good. It remained tightly shut. He leaned against the wall. Shaun knew that there was no escape this way. He would have to go back down the stairs, return to Billy's prison.

Carefully, quietly, he crept down the stairs. He went slowly. He could not afford to make a sound.

The door was open now and Shaun could see right into the room. Billy was lying on the floor and the man in the suit was kneeling beside him, tying the boy's hands together behind his back. He turned the boy over and immediately Billy started telling the men what would happen to them if they didn't let him go. He told them that his teachers would be looking for him and they'd better look out, but the man laughed, a horrible sinister laugh, and thrust a gag in Billy's mouth. Then he pushed him roughly against the wall, as if he were a bundle of old clothes.

"Careful," the bogus duke warned him "I don't want anyone hurt."

"You better watch out you don't get hurt yourself," the other man spat at him. "It's your stupid greed that's brought him here in the first place. Get rid of those kids though Pete. We must have everyone off the premises by ten past five. That's the deadline. We're not going to let anyone upset that, certainly not a bunch of school kids."

"Don't worry," the third man told him. "I'll go and tell the driver that the boy's mother came and fetched him, that her husband had had an accident and she'd had to come for him and leave immediately."

"But what's going to happen when the coach gets back

27

to the school and finds that's not true?" queried the bogus duke.

"Don't look for trouble," Pete said coolly. "The coach will be late getting back to the school. It will have a puncture a mile down the road. There's a long walk to go and get help."

"It was a good job you British built your castles in such out of the way places," the foreign man said and he gave the same evil sounding laugh. "Now to business. Pete, we will need two wheelbarrows now. We have two bodies. We will take the boy with us. I know you don't want him hurt," he added as he saw the older man was about to interrupt," but it might not be such a bad thing to have a duke and a child. We might get a bigger ransom for their release."

"They pay well for children," the bogus duke said.

The foreigner turned on him and said venomously, "I don't like children. I hate children. Children always get in the way."

The three men talked amongst themselves for a while. They were talking more quietly now and Shaun could not follow their conversation, he could only pick up the odd word or two. He had to do something to help. He was the only one who knew what was happening. He had to get help, but how?

The two men came out of the room, the bogus duke and the other man who looked like a gardener and who must be Peter. Shaun thought they were making for the spiral staircase. He looked round him in despair. There was no **chance of escape.** There was no time to get back up the stairs. He started to edge backwards. He need not have bothered. The two men didn't even look in his direction. They went past the bottom of the staircase and along the dark tunnel beyond it.

The foreigner stayed in the room, he turned his back on the door and, started to sort out the silver that the bogus duke had taken.

This was Shaun's chance of escape. If the two men had gone along the tunnel, there must be another way out. Slowly, carefully, he descended the stairs, watching the man in the

28

Suddenly he was through it, standing in a circle of light.

room, frightened that at any second, he would look up and see him. He needn't have worried. The man was too busy gloating over the contents of that sack.

Shaun had only gone a few steps along the tunnel, when he was engulfed in darkness again. He had to feel his way carefully along the wall. The ground was uneven and cobbled and Shaun had to move cautiously, praying he would not trip over one of the protruding stones. There was no sign of the men in front of him, no flash of torchlight, no sound of footsteps on the cobbled ground. He seemed to be walking into a dark wall of silence and suddenly he was through it, standing in a circle of light as if he was being shown up by the footlights on a stage. It took a second or two for his eyes to become accustomed to the glare. Then he realised the light was coming from above him and looking up, he saw he was looking up at a circle of sky. The men must have climbed up this way and he started to look round for footholds in the stone wall, but he couldn't find any. He dug his fingers into the narrow gaps between the stones and tried to pull himself up only to slither back to his starting point. The walls were dark and slippery. He was as much a prisoner here as he had been in that dark cupboard behind the glass wall. There must be a way out. The men had disappeared. Perhaps there was an exit from further back in the tunnel that he had missed. Shaun started back the way he had come, feeling along the walls, stopping every so often to listen, fearful that the foreign man would come along the passage before he had found a way to escape.

Mr Clark had collected all the other children in a group outside the castle. He was worried about the two lost boys but he did not want the rest of the group to know his feelings.

"I told you all to stay together but it seems Billy and Shaun have taken it on themselves to wander off somewhere," he said. "I want them back here and I want them now. So we will divide into groups and have a quick search of the grounds. If you see them tell them to come back here and if they won't come, you come straight back and tell me. Now Dean, how many in your group? Well you five can go down to the adventure playground and look there. Follow the sign posts. They'll show you where to go. Alison and Mary and, alright Emma as well, you three look in the garden where the statues are. Joanne and Julie, you go down the drive and up to the front of the castle."

As soon as everyone had been given their area, Mr.Clark made them synchronize their watches.

"Now, I want everyone back at two thirty five. That gives you twenty minutes and not a second more. Right off you go."

The children ran off. It was all part of the adventure to them. The two teachers discussed the situation. They were both worried about the boys, worried and cross.

The children started to return and Mrs Dixon lined them all up and started to count them.

"There's two missing," she announced and the panic was rising in her voice. "There are two short."

"We know there are," Mr Clark said patiently.

"No, there's another two gone. Joanne's not here. Joanne and Julie, where are they?" and she started to run towards the drive.

Mr Clark ran after her. "You stay here," he said shortly. "I'll see if they're there."

There was no sign of either girl in the drive but the duke and one of the gardeners were talking in front of the castle entrance. They must have seen the girls and he started walking towards them. Immediately the gardener turned and came to meet him.

"I think one of your children is missing," he said. "I've been looking for you to tell you. His mother came. Bennet she said her name was, said her husband had had an accident and she had to take her son with her."

"Oh, oh thank you," Mr Clark said. "We'd been looking for him."

"I'd left the message with the duke but he's just told me he hadn't found you to let you know."

"I think one of your children is missing".

"Thank you very much, "Mr Clark said. "We'll be getting the children back now. We're late already."

"Get the children back," he told Mrs Dixon when he reached the terrace. "There's something mighty odd going on here," and he told her the message he'd been given by the gardener.

"But Billy Bennet hasn't got a father," Mrs Dixon said.

"I know that and you know that but they obviously don't. They've got the boy somewhere haven't they? How else would they have known his name, but they only mentioned the one boy so where's Shaun?"

"And where are the girls?"

"Come on. We're taking the children back to the coach and acting as if nothing is wrong. There's someone looking at us from that window up there. I've just seen the curtain move. We're getting out of here and we're getting help. Look I've written my friend's name and telephone number on this. I play squash with him. He's a policeman, plain clothes, but he's still a policeman. He'll know what to do. Tell him everything and make sure it's Mike you speak to. Anyone else might try to fob you off. Just tell him everything that's happened. Tell him to park out on the road and as soon as I see him, I'll go out."

"Why? What are you going to do?"

"I'm staying here. There's four children here, remember? I don't want anyone to know I'm staying, so I'll get on to the coach and jump off when we start to move."

The gardener stood at the edge of the car park, piling rubbish into his wheelbarrow. He watched the children file into the coach and saw it move out. He hurried back to the castle, not waiting long enough to see Mr Clark jump out of the door and throw himself on to the ground behind some bushes.

Chapter Five

Joanne and Julie had run off towards the drive.

"They're not here," Joanne said, "I'll go and look down the well," and she ran across to the circular stone wall. "Here Julie," she called, turning round, "there's a ladder here. Come and look."

Julie went and joined her friend.

"I bet they're down there," Joanne said, "it's just the sort of place where Billy Bennet would go. Let's go down and see."

"Sh, listen," Julie put her hand on Joanne's arm. "There's someone down there. I can hear them talking."

"I bet it's Billy and Shaun."

"No" Julie said, shaking her head. "I can hear a man's voice. I think it's two men talking."

Both girls were whispering now. They didn't know why but some feeling inside them was warning them to be quiet.

"Look at the ladder," Joanne whispered. "It's shaking. They're coming up."

"Don't let them see us."

"Get behind those bushes, quick."

The girls ran to the other side of the drive and crouched behind the bushes.

"Lie down, get down low," Joanne hissed at her friend.

A head appeared over the edge of the low wall, a man's head. He looked around and then clambered out of the well. Turning round, he helped another, fatter man to climb out.

"That's the duke," Julie said.

"What's he doing down the well?"

"I don't know."

The duke brushed his clothes down and then the gardener turned a wheel that was fastened at the side of the ladder.

"My uncle's got a ladder like that in his loft," Julie whispered. "It's a folding ladder and you turn that wheel and it folds itself up in sections."

The two men stood talking beside the well, then they turned and started to walk towards the castle. The girls waited, not daring to move. The men went round the side of the castle. The girls waited for a few more minutes to make sure that they were not coming back and, when there was no sign of them, they ran across to the well.

"Billy," Joanne called down the well.

"Sh..h, they might hear you," Julie said looking towards the castle, and certainly the sound of Joanne's voice echoed back at them from the well seeming to grow louder and louder, covering them in a cloud of sound.

"I'm going down," Joanne said, beginning to turn the wheel on the ladder, leaning over the wall to watch the rungs unfold.

"We ought to be back at the terrace by now. You know what Mr Clark said.."

"I won't be a minute. You keep watch," and Joanne clambered over the low wall and started to descend the ladder. She had hardly disappeared from sight when the two men came back round the castle, the gardener wheeling a barrow.

"Joanne, they're coming back," she said as loudly as she dared but there was no answering voice. Whatever was she going to do? The men were walking towards the well. They were sure to see her, if they hadn't done so already. She crouched down. If only she could get across the drive without them seeing her. Then she heard the men speaking and looking over the top of the wall, she saw that they had turned to talk to another man. This was her chance and she dashed across the drive and threw herself headlong on the grass behind the bushes, expecting to hear one of the men shouting at her. But no shout came. She looked through the foliage and saw that the two men were coming on down the drive and the man to whom they had been talking was walking away. They had been talking to Mr Clark. She could see that now. She wanted to call out to him, to run after him but this voice deep inside her urged her to stay hidden.

The two men had reached the well.

"I thought you'd wound this thing up," the gardener grumbled.

"So I did."

"Well you didn't get it up far enough," and he started to turn the wheel.

"Come and give me a hand," he said. It didn't sound like a gardener talking to a duke.

The two men lifted the ladder from the well and balanced it across the wheelbarrow. It was obviously very heavy and the men puffed and panted as they lifted it. They wheeled the barrow back towards the castle. Julie sat on the grass and watched them. She didn't know what to do. How could Joanne get out of the well now and why hadn't she climbed out when the men started to lift the ladder. She must get across to the well and find out, if only those men would hurry. But they didn't hurry. They lifted the ladder from the barrow and rested it against the castle wall. Then they stood and talked. Then the gardener started back down the drive pushing his wheelbarrow. He walked within a few feet of Julie. She waited until he was out of sight and ran across to the well.

"Joanne," she called down the shaft, "Joanne," but there was no reply. She called again and again but there was no answer. Something was wrong. Something had happened to her friend. She must fetch help. Julie ran as fast as she could back towards the terrace. Mr Clark would know what to do, but he wasn't there. No-one was there. The terrace was empty, empty and silent. Julie stared about her with numbed horror. Where was everyone? She had to find them. She had to get help. Forgetting all about caution, she ran across the lawns, down towards the coach. She would wait for them there.

The coach wasn't there. Julie stared at the empty car park in disbelief. The coach must be here. They wouldn't go without her. She stood there not knowing what to do, feeling very alone in that empty place, alone and frightened. She walked across the tarmac, and down the bank on to the road and there was the coach showing up like a bright ladybird on a sycamore leaf, reflecting the rays of the afternoon sun. Julie could have wept with relief at the sight of it and then she realised it was going away from her, away from the castle and Joanne down the well. It was winding its way down the narrow lane beneath the castle leaving her behind. It could only have left a few minutes before. Julie ran along the middle of the road, shouting after it, but the coach went steadily on. No-one had seen her. She stood there and stared after it. Whatever was she going to do? She was alone and she had to get help to find Joanne. Julie was suddenly overcome with despair. She sat on the grass bank and burst into tears. She started as someone shook her shoulder.

"Julie," it was Mr Clark. "Julie, you're alright. Come away from the road."

She followed him through the trees and settled down behind a stone wall.

"We've got to rescue Joanne," she burst out. "She's down the well."

Mr Clark looked startled.

"She's fallen into the well?" he asked.

"No, she went down the ladder," and she told the teacher all about them hearing voices down the well and how the men climbed up the ladder and how Joanne had climbed down it to see what was at the bottom and how the men came back

Julie stared at the empty car park in disbelief.

38

and had taken the ladder away and when she went and shouted down the well there was no answer and she might be drowning and Julie burst into tears again.

"Did the men look wet when they came out of the well?" Mr Clark asked.

"No," Julie said doubtfully.

"Then I think you can rest assured that Joanne is not drowning. It sounds as if that well is a blind well. There's probably a passage down there that no-one wants you to know about. I think we'll wait here until help arrives," and he told Julie how the telephones didn't work and how Mrs Johnstone had gone for help.

"I don't expect anyone to be here for half an hour at least. Come on, we'll go and wait nearer the road."

The two of them waited beneath a willow tree. The drooping branches almost swept the ground and provided a curtain which hid them from view. The time of waiting seemed to go on for ever. At first Julie had been impatient and wanted to go and try to rescue Joanne immediately and she tried to make Mr Clark move but he grunted and leaned against the trunk of the tree and started to clean out his pipe. Then Julie began to worry and, despite the heat of the day, she felt suddenly cold, cold and worried. She began to shiver. Mr Clark took off his jacket and put it round her shoulders. He told her stories and she must have fallen asleep.

She had not seen the car arrive and park on the road beneath them. Mr Clark told her to follow him and he skirted the car park, keeping beneath the shadow of the trees.

Mr Clark opened the back door of the car and he and Julie climbed in and sat on the back seat. Julie could not see the driver's face. He seemed to be staring out of the windscreen and did not turn to look at them.

"You were quick," Mr Clark said.

"I thought I'd better be," the man replied, "Your lady friend was very explicit."

"And very worried."

"That too, but she gave me some interesting informa-

39

tion. She said she'd caught a glimpse of the duke and she didn't think it was the real one. She thought this man was wearing make-up and had a wig on. That interested us. You see the duchess had phoned us earlier to say that the duke had not phoned her at mid-day as arranged and she had been unable to get through to him on the phone. British Telecom insist there is no fault on the line but there's something wrong with the one at the castle. I was just going to send someone up to have a look when your message came through. It seemed a little further investigation was needed. Put me in the picture."

Mr Clark told him exactly what had happened on the trip.

The man in the front of the car spread a map out on the empty front seat. Julie could see that it was a map of the castle.

"When was the boy last seen?" he asked.

Mr Clark pointed out the spot on the map.

"And the second boy?"

"And the girl?"

They sat in silence for a few minutes while the man in the front of the car studied the map.

"Why doesn't he go and get Joanne out of the well. Why does he just sit there like that?" Julie wanted to urge him to do something. She looked at Mr Clark but he was sitting back in the car seat looking relaxed and untroubled.

Then a man in a navy track suit was opening the front door and, lifting the maps from the seat. He slid into the car. "There is no-one in the main part of the castle. There are three or four men in the cellars. I've left two men on watch but I don't think they intend to return to the main part of the building. The front doors are locked. We've left the window open round the back."

"We'd better set up headquarters in the castle?"

"It would be the safest. They might come up to the ground floor but I suggest we use this room here," and he pointed out a place on the map. "Reception's good. Visibility's good and there's a room at the back there where you can make a cup of tea" he added with a grin.

"Right," said the driver and he reached forward and lifted a microphone from a rest and started to speak into it. Everything about him was unhurried, his movements, his speech and Julie wanted to urge him to hurry but there was something about him that warned her not to interfere.

He was giving instructions, guiding them to the well, telling them to bring Joanne to the castle when they found her. Then he asked the man in the front seat to get Julie and Mr Clark into the castle. He was going to get his car out of sight.

"Follow me," the man said and started to lead them through the trees, away from the castle. He was almost trotting and Julie had to run to keep up with him. They went in a circle and when they came to the edge of the trees again, they were facing the castle from the other side.

"I'm carrying you across here," he told Julie curtly. "We've got to move quickly," and before Julie had time to reply, he had hoisted her over his shoulders and was running across the grass. Julie hardly knew what was happening. She knew they were inside the castle but the man seemed to be running and did not attempt to put her down. Then he stopped and she slid slowly to the ground and the man steadied her while she regained her balance. Mr Clark followed them in. He was red faced and out of breath.

"God, you set a pace didn't you?"

The man grinned. "Keep away from the window," he said. "Mike'll be here," and he went silently out of the room.

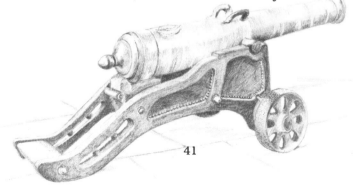

41

Chapter Six

Joanne had climbed slowly down the last rungs of the extended ladder, letting her eyes adjust to the darkness as she went further into the well. Her foot touched the cobbled ground and she leaned a hand on the damp wall to regain her balance. She was surprised that there was no water at the bottom of the well. She looked up at the circle of brilliant light above her. It seemed a long way away but it still made the area around her appear very dark and it took a while for her eyes to become accustomed to the dim light.

"What did those men want to come down here for," she thought. Then she saw the dark shadow in the wall opposite her. She went towards it and was swallowed up by the shadow, for it was a tunnel leading out from the base of the well and, as she took a few steps along it, she was covered by a blanket of darkness and silence. For a moment she felt bewildered and lost. She turned back the way she had come and saw the lighter arch that showed where the tunnel reached the well and she stumbled towards it.

Then she heard the ladder shaking. Someone was coming down. Julie must have got tired of waiting up there on her own and was coming down to see if she could see her.

She didn't see her friend. What she did see was the ladder beginning to move as the sections were folding upwards. Someone was folding the ladder in. She threw herself at it, leaping at the bottom rung to try and hold it back. Her fingers touched the section but failed to hold it. She leapt towards it again but the ladder was moving steadily upwards and was out of her reach. She stared at it with horror, watching her means of escape going further and further away from her.

"Joanne," a voice behind her whispered her name. Swinging round, she found herself facing Shaun. He put his finger to his lips, warning her to be quiet.

"Come in here," he said, motioning to the tunnel, "In case they look down and see us. They're bad men. I thought I heard a voice - that's why I came through. How did you get down?"

Joanne told him how Mr Clark had sent them to look for the boys and how she had seen the ladder and climbed down to see what was at the bottom of the well and how someone had wound it up again, "But Julie knows I'm down here. I'm sure she'll get help. Where's Billy?"

"They've got him," Shaun said and told Joanne everything that had happened and how Billy was tied up in the room at the end of the tunnel.

"We've got to go and rescue him," Joanne said.

"But how?" asked Shaun. "Even if we did get him away there's no way we can get out ourselves," and he told Joanne how he had battled to force the door open at the top of the spiral stairs.

"Perhaps I can find a way," Joanne said.

So the two of them crept along the dark passage and climbed the spiral stairs. They went carefully past the half open door that lead to the room where Billy was imprisoned, but the man was bent over the table studying pieces of silver he was taking from the sack and every so often he laughed, a horrible sound that frightened Joanne. The two children climbed the spiral staircase and Shaun explained how the secret door had opened from the outside, but, try as they might, neither of them could get it to budge an inch. They gave up at last and sat on the floor to discuss their predicament.

"I think we'd better make our way back down to the well," Joanne said. "Julie knows I went down that and that's where she'll be looking for me."

So the two of them started their cautious journey back down the spiral stairs and along the dark tunnel. They had to wait for some time at the bottom of the stairs because the man inside was moving around a lot and muttering to himself and they thought he might look up and see them as they passed the door, but he quietened down again and Shaun and Joanne crept past the room and started going along the tunnel, feeling their way cautiously along the wall. They were about half way along when Joanne was suddenly seized from behind and before she could cry out, a hand was pressed across her mouth. Shaun was siezed in the same way but Joanne didn't know that. They were both too shocked and startled to cry out.

A voice whispered in Joanne's ear, "We are not going to hurt you. We are taking you back to the surface. I am going to put you over my shoulder and carry you but you must keep quiet. When I take my hand away from your mouth, you must not utter a sound. Nod if you understand."

The man had to repeat the message before Joanne fully took it in and then she nodded. The following few minutes were the worst of the day. She was hoisted over this man's shoulder like a bag of coal and she was being bumped up and down as the man ran along the tunnel. Then she seemed to be passed from one person to another as she was lifted out of the well and then she was being carried again. She lost all idea of place and direction then. The only thing that seemed to fill her mind was the man's order, you must not make a sound - and although she wanted to shout out, she kept her lips firmly shut. She shut her eyes too, for the world seemed to be going round and round and she didn't know where she was. Then she was being lowered to the ground and, opening her eyes, she found she was in one of the castle rooms and Mr

She was hoisted over the man's shoulder like a bag of coal.

Clark was sitting in a chair cleaning out his pipe and Julie was beside him. Then another man came into the room and put Shaun down on the floor beside her. The man who had brought Joanne out of the tunnel pushed the woollen helmet back on his head.

"There's two of your chickens home to roost," he said.

"Thanks Mike," Mr Clark said. "Is there any sign of Billy?"

"I hope our two friends can tell us that, " Mike said and he started asking Joanne and Shaun questions. Julie tried to interrupt. She wanted to know what had happened to Joanne but Mr Clark told her to be quiet. Slowly at first, then more swiftly as he became more confident, Shaun told Mike everything that had happened. When he said that the foreign man had said ten past five was the zero hour, Mike looked at his watch and said that they did not have much time. Then he started talking into the microphone on one of the machines that another man had brought into the room. He was giving orders. There was a lot of crackling on the machine and then the children could hear other voices answering him but it was difficult to hear what they were saying. Then he turned back to Shaun and was asking about the men he had seen. There was nothing gentle about his questioning now. He was curt and blunt and Shaun answered as quickly as he could. When he described the man with the foreign accent, Mike grunted.

"I had a gut feeling we were dealing with that gang," he said.

He turned towards Mr Clark.

"There's a group that have been responsible for a number of kidnappings on the continent. We were told they'd slipped into Britain but we'd lost track of them. We've put guards on several people we thought were at risk including some of the Royal family purely as a precaution. I think they're in for a couple of surprises this time. They're going to find the duke isn't as wealthy as the industrialists they generally attack, and secondly they're going to find out we don't put up with that sort of thing in Britain."

He pulled his mask casually down over his face. Mike didn't seem to hurry over anything and yet there was something about him you did not question.

"Keep the children away from the window," he said as he slipped out of the door.

There was silence for a few seconds when he had gone, then all three children started talking at once. They had so much to tell each other. In the end Mr Clark put his hands over his ears and suggested they went through to the other room to see if they could make a cup of tea, but they had hardly had time to go through the door when the whole building began to shake and a roaring noise filled the room, a noise that repeated itself like a mechanical digger, growing louder and louder, echoing back from every corner of that high ceilinged room. The noise became so overpowering that the walls seemed to shake and Joanne and Julie ran back into the room in alarm. Whatever was happening?

Mr Clark put his hands over his ears.

Chapter Seven

Meanwhile, in the cellar beneath the castle, the crooks were beginning to move. The bogus duke had joined the foreign man in the room where the real duke and Billy were imprisoned and they had been sorting out the loot that had been in the sack. They were so preoccupied with what they were doing that they did not notice the time. They froze and stared at each other with horror when they heard something moving outside the door. There were three short taps. The foreign man stepped silently towards the heavy door.

"Who is there?", he asked softly.

"It's me, Pete."

"You are before time," the man said, letting him into the room.

"I know that but there isn't a soul in the place. The old lady went off early and the girls went off soon after three, as soon as they cleared up after that school trip, and old Thompson won't turn up till after half past five. We're laughing."

"The teacher believed your story about the boy's mother coming?' the bogus duke asked anxiously.

"Swallowed it like a lamb. We needn't worry about

them."

"We can do with the extra time, now that we have two bodies," the foreigner said. "Have you got two barrows."

"Outside in the passage as arranged," the gardener said shortly.

"Come on then, we will get the duke ready for his journey," and he laughed, the evil laugh that had frightened Billy.

The bogus duke began packing silver into the sack but, with a curse, the foreign man told him to come and help.

"He's a dead weight," he said as they tried to drag the unconscious duke out into the passage and hoist him into the wheelbarrow.

The fat man winced at the word 'dead' and started to say something but then saw the look on the foreign man's face, that silenced him. It took all their effort to get the recumbent duke into the barrow. Then the gardener covered him with dead leaves from a sack. It was difficult to imagine that there was a body beneath them.

"We will still work to the plan," the foreigner said curtly.

"Take the wheelbarrow to the terrace as we arranged, so that it looks as though you are taking the usual garden rubbish. Make sure there is no one about to see you. If the coast is clear, return and fetch us. If you are not alone, put out that white cloth and abort the trip."

"O.K., O.K." the gardener said. "We've been through it all a thousand times and I'll tell you this. There's no garden rubbish that weighs a fraction of this load here." He pushed the barrow along the tunnel and up the slope to the garden.

While he was gone the other two men began packing items of silver into the sacks. They discarded some of the larger pieces leaving them on the table.

"We have only the three minutes to load everything," the foreigner said. "There will not be much time. We will not have time for all."

The sack was heavy enough as it was, and it took the two of them to lift it into the wheelbarrow in the passage. Then they went back and picked up Billy and put him in the barrow too, alongside the sack. Billy had heard every word the men had said but he pretended he hadn't. He pretended to be fast asleep. He did not want those men to inject him like they had injected the duke. He found it hard to keep his eyes shut or stop himself from shouting out because the men carried him more roughly than they had handled their sack of treasure. He had never felt so uncomfortable in his life. His legs and arms were alternately painful and numb from the rope that tied them and, if he tried to move, those bonds seemed to tighten and send shooting pains through his whole body. The worst thing of all was the gag in his mouth. He thought it was going to suffocate him when the man first pushed it into his mouth, but, after those first few minutes of panic had subsided, he found that if he kept his teeth clenched he could hold the evil tasting cloth at the front of his mouth and leave his throat and air passage clear.

Where were they taking him? What was going to happen now?

"Cover him up," the foreigner said.

"We needn't bother," the bogus duke told him. "Pete said there's no one about."

"Cover him."

Billy was immediately covered with damp, mouldering leaves. For a moment he thought they were going to stop him breathing. They covered his eyes and filled his nostrils but he blew hard through his nose and they cleared a little. Then the two men started pushing the wheelbarrow. It was dreadful. They were going over cobbles and every stone, every bump reverberated through Billy's body. The two men were arguing but Billy hardly realized what they were saying, he was so uncomfortable.

"There is not the need to hurry. We have plenty of time. This we have planned to the second. There will be no mistake," the foreign man said, and even Billy beneath his pile of leaves could sense the evil in the man's voice.

It was at that precise moment that they heard the

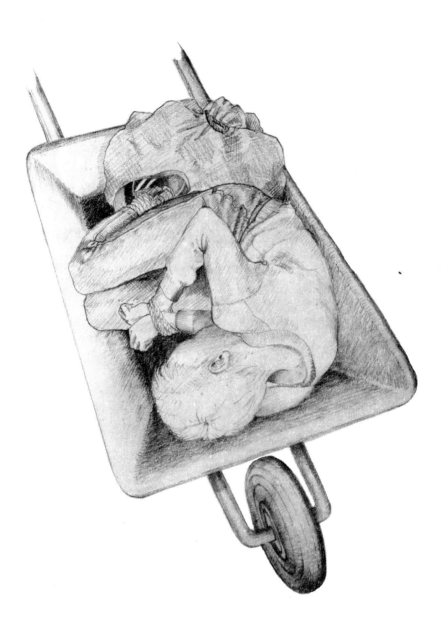

...... picked up Billy and put him in the barrow too, alongside the sack.

51

roaring noise. Both men stopped momentarily and stared at each other. The roaring was growing louder, developing into a mechanical beat which echoed all round them, seeming to come at them from every corner of those dark passages, reverberating through them so fiercely that they shook the walls.

The man cursed in his own language. Instinctively both men had started to run, the foreigner pushing the wheelbarrow in front of him, jolting it over the cobbles without a thought for the boy hidden in it.

Billy had heard the roaring. It sounded like a train bearing down on them. Almost immediately he was being tossed around, being bumped and rolled like a piece of flotsam on a rough sea. At every movement his bonds seemed to be cutting more deeply into his flesh. Then he was jolted to a stop and he felt himself sliding.

"What are you doing?"

"The wheel's stuck in these rails. Come and give me a hand."

"I can't lift that side round. Quick. Lift."

"I can't - it's stuck."

"Leave it then. There's no time. They will not wait," and the foreigner began to run towards the end of the tunnel.

The gardener had begun returning to the tunnel when he heard the roaring sound. At first he was undecided what to do. Should he go back to the terrace where he had left the unconscious duke or should he return to the others. He must fetch them. The important thing was not to panic and he ran down the slope to the tunnel entrance, meeting the foreigner coming out of the tunnel.

"Where's the boy?" he asked.

"There's no time. We have three minutes from when they land. They will not wait. We have the duke. That is what we came for."

"Hold hard," the gardener said, standing in front of him and stopping him going by, "You take the boy. He knows too much. He could recognise me. If you want me to cover up here, you make sure they don't leave without the boy. Do you understand?"

The foreigner nodded.

"You make sure of it then or I'll blow everything." He had taken hold of the man's arm and he shook it violently. The man pulled his arm away and started running up the slope towards the terrace.

The gardener ran into the tunnel. The wheelbarrow was right on its side now and the bogus duke was frantically trying to push some silver back into the sack. Greed was written all over his face. He had no interest in the boy or the other members of the gang. He was thinking only of the value of the silver. The gardener shouldered him aside and heaved Billy over his shoulder.

"You'd better leave that lot behind," he said to the other man, "you'll be left behind yourself if you don't get a move on," and he started to run in the same direction as the foreigner.

The bogus duke looked after him in an undecided way. He pushed a few last pieces into the sack, then heaving it over his shoulder, he began to run in the same direction.

Meanwhile, back in the castle, the children had been silenced by the sudden and overpowering noise.

"It's a helicopter," said Shaun, running towards the window, "It's a helicopter. It's going round and round the castle."

The two girls ran towards him.

"Get back from the window," Mr Clark called out. "Get right back."

The children stood back a few steps but they leaned round the curtain, anxious to see everything that was going on.

"It's slowed down," Shaun said. "Look - its rotor blades are slowing down. It's hovering. It's going to land."

"It's going to land on the terrace," Mr Clark said He was just as excited as the children, "but keep back. You know what Mike said."

They saw the helicopter settle on the ground and the

door in the side slide open. At the same moment, the foreigner dashed from the side path and across the grass to the machine. The children could see that he was shouting and waving his arms excitedly but they couldn't hear what he was saying. A man jumped out of the helicopter and ran across to the wheelbarrow. The two men started to push it towards the helicopter.

"That's that foreign man," Shaun had shouted, "the one that tied Billy up."

"It's a pretty heavy load of leaves," Mr Clark said, "if it needs the two of them to push it."

The two men had reached the shadow of the helicopter and were brushing the leaves onto the ground with their hands when the gardener came round the castle, trotting towards the machine with Billy over his shoulder.

"That's Bill," Shaun shouted. "We've got to get him back. We've got to. Look they're putting him in the helicopter. They're kidnapping him. We've got to stop them. Come on," and he made a dash for the door but Mr Clark caught hold of him and told him to stay exactly where he was.

The four of them stood there, standing back from the window but able to see everything that was going on. The crooks seemed to be having it all their own way.

"Where's Mike?" Mr Clark muttered anxiously. "What's he up to?"

The two bodies had been stowed into the helicopter. The pilot was already back in it and pulling the foreigner in behind him. The man who had acted the part of the duke had appeared now and was dragging the sack behind him. He looked red faced and was puffing. He shouted when he saw the foreigner getting into the helicopter, saw the rotor blades begin to move. The man in the helicopter shouted back at him. He began to run, still dragging the sack behind him, but carelessly now. Pieces of silver began to spill from the sack as he ran. The foreigner was shouting now. The rotor blades were gathering speed. They were not going to wait for him. With a despairing shout, he flung the sack aside and raced

54

towards the helicopter but at that instant it began to lift from the ground.

At the same moment there was another shout and the gardener ran out on to the grass. He had obviously intended to stay behind and had wheeled the empty barrow back on to the gravel path but now he was shouting and pointing towards the sky. Another helicopter had appeared and was coming in their direction and it was coming fast, buzzing like an angry gnat. The crooks could not see it but the gardener could see the danger. The pilot had swung his machine round. He had seen the danger too. The bogus duke had made a desperate dash for the machine and had grasped the sill of the doorway. He had neither the breath nor the strength to pull himself in and for a few seconds he was suspended in

For a few seconds he was suspended in the air.

the air as the helicopter lifted from the ground but that was as far as it could lift for the dark blue helicopter was hovering above it, preventing it from going any higher. The crook's helicopter tried to move forwards, then sideways but the smaller machine buzzed above it the whole time, not giving it time to manoeuvre. At times the two machines were so close together that the children, watching from the castle, thought they were going to crash.

The foreigner jumped out of the helicopter. He fell heavily and limped to one side. The man who had come in the helicopter jumped after him. Both men took guns from their jackets and started to fire them at the helicopter above them. The children saw a flash as a gun fired.

"They're going to kill them," Julie cried.

"They'll crash."

"Get right back, right back."

The fat man who had acted the part of the duke had fallen from the helicopter and lain on the ground for a few seconds. Now he too had taken a gun from his pocket and was aiming at the buzzing helicopter.

"That's Billy's water pistol," Shaun said in disbelief. "That's not a real gun."

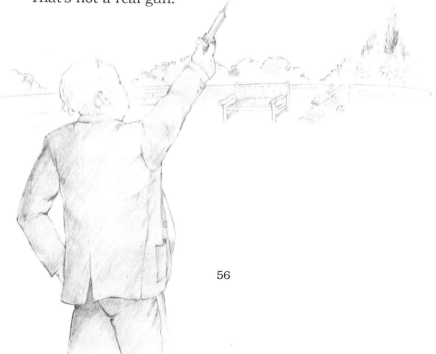

Sure enough a jet of water squirted out of the gun when the man pressed the trigger but he hardly noticed because at that moment he was seized by one of the black helmeted men who had crept up behind him. He had moved so stealthily that even the children from their good vantage point had not noticed him.

The foreigner tried to fire again but nothing happened. He shook his gun and aimed it again but still it wouldn't fire. He tossed it away with an exclamation of anger and ran across towards the drive but as he reached the gravel another one of the men who had rescued Joanne and Shaun rugby tackled him and felled him to the ground.

The other man who was shooting had run out of ammunition too. He looked around him. Two more of Mike's team were approaching him, cautiously. They obviously expected trouble but the man admitted defeat. He tossed his gun away and shrugged his shoulders, allowing the two men to lead him away.

The crooks' helicopter was on the ground now and the rotors were slowing. The other machine landed beside it.

Everything happened so quickly then. The three children were cheering and Mr Clark was laughing.

"Come on," he said, "let's go and find Billy."

They saw the duke first, the real duke, lying unconscious on the ground. Then they saw Billy. The ropes had been cut and there were angry red weals where they had cut into his flesh. Mike was kneeling beside him massaging his ankles. The boy looked tired and pale but he grinned when he saw his friends.

"Where's Henrietta?" he asked.

Chapter Eight

It all seemed such an anti-climax. The five crooks sat in a dejected group guarded by two of the black clad men who had rescued Shaun and Joanne. Their faces were still blackened and the hoods pulled down over their heads. They laughed and chatted as if they were on a trip out. You wouldn't have thought they had just caught some of the most wanted men in Europe.

The prisoners were handcuffed and looked subdued except for the foreign man. He spat at the children when he saw them and muttered at them in a different language.

"I hate children," he spat at them, "I detest children. Children mean trouble."

"They did in your case mate," one of the guards said, "now shut up and be quiet."

He was a little quieter but he muttered and scowled at the children. Julie was pleased when a dark van drew up and three of the hand-cuffed men were taken across to it. The gardener and the fat man had to wait until a police car drove up and two policemen took them away. They went without any trouble, not like the other three men. They had shouted and struggled and tried to kick the guards and the men had to come across from the helicopters to help get them into the van. Even as it drove away, the children could hear the prisoners shouting and bumping against the sides.

Mike and one of his men had been massaging Billy's wrists and ankles, to get the circulation flowing again. A doctor arrived and examined both Billy and the duke. He said that they were fine but he'd like them in hospital for the night just to make sure there were no side effects. He wouldn't let Billy move although he insisted he felt alright.

"You won't when you start moving," he told him curtly, "not when you've had your legs tied as tightly as that."

Billy was looking happier altogether. Someone had found his bag and Henrietta was nosing up his sleeve. Sandwiches and cakes and cups of coffee were being handed round.

Mike came over and made them listen. He had something he had to tell them. He didn't tell them who the three crooks were who had planned to kidnap the duke but he did say they were wanted by several countries on the continent but we didn't want them in England. What was more, they didn't want anyone to ever know they had been in England, that their friends would try and take revenge if they thought we were responsible for their capture.

"By the time you get home," he told the children,"they will be back in Italy where they belong and the Italian police can have the credit of capturing them. The two British men that were mixed up with them will be charged with burglary and no-one must ever know that they planned anything else except that, so I've got to ask you to do something very difficult. Keep what has happened today to yourselves. You can discuss it with your parents. One of us will be round to explain the situation to them tonight, but after that you must forget that today ever happened. I want each one of you to promise that you will keep it a secret."

He looked at each of the children in turn and each one nodded at him.

"You too, Steve," he said looking at Mr Clark.

"I should think you know me by now."

"I want that promise from you too."

"You have it."

It was at that moment that the ambulance arrived. The men insisted on putting Billy on a stretcher and carrying him out to the ambulance although he said he felt alright. The others came over to see him off. Billy looked important sitting there on the stretcher.

"You can go and see him tomorrow," Mike told them.

"I'll go down to the hospital with him," Mr Clark said, that's if you'd er... em......"

"Get these three home," Mike said, "of course I will. That's if they don't mind going in the helicopter."

"Gee whiz," said Shaun.

Billy started to push the blankets off his legs.

"I can go with them," he said, "I feel alright now. I..", but the ambulance man had shut the door firmly and as the ambulance drew away, they could hear Billy grumbling, "it isn't fair," he was saying, "it isn't right. It was me who got tied up but they're having all the fun."

I hope you have enjoyed the story and will come to visit my home Belvoir Castle one day. When you do come you must remember that many of the lovely things you see are precious and fragile and have been in my family for many years. So, please do not try to touch any of them, they will not reveal any hidden secret passages.

The Duke of Rutland.